PART & PARCEL

A SHORT SCIENCE FICTION STORY

SUPER GREAT CHALLENGE STORIES
BOOK 11

RYAN M. WILLIAMS

Visit our website at ryanmwilliams.com

Glittering Throng Press

PO BOX 179

RAINIER WA 98576-0179

eBook ISBN-13: 978-1-946440-98-3

Paperback ISBN-13: 978-1-946440-99-0

GTP NO. 53
SGC NO. 11

ACKNOWLEDGMENTS

This story is one of 52 weekly stories written (and published) over a year. It's part of the Super Great Challenge (SGC) run by Dean Wesley Smith and Kristine Kathryn Rusch through the WMG Publishing workshops on Teachable. Without that challenge, this story (and the others) likely wouldn't exist.

Additionally, in creating the cover art for the stories in the SGC, I've typically used Blender—my **favorite application ever**—an open source, free, 3D modeling, digital painting, animation, sculpting, and video editing application. I've taken courses and watched tutorials from creators like Ducky 3D, Southern-Shotty, Grant Abbitt, Curtis Holt, Ryan King, the Blender Studio, CG Cookie, CG Boost, the Blender Guru and so many others. It's a wonderful and inspiring community.

And I'm so grateful for the **support of my members** on my site (ryanmwilliams.com) for their encouragement for this challenge. My family has also been instrumental in making this possible. It helps immensely having people behind me on this journey. Thank you.

———

CHAPTER 1
THE CRIME SCENE

A grisly scene greeted Detectives Wood and Stone after they pushed past the street cops into the abandoned storefront on Shore street, down near the old port. The call came in at 7:33 AM, passed to them before Zack Wood even had a chance at something approximating coffee. The air smelled rank with decay and low tide. A brisk breeze came off the water and low boiling gray clouds choked the sky. Even the seagulls on the rotting piers looked dejected this morning. He took a final breath of the fetid air outside, knowing it was likely to smell fresh compared to whatever they had to look at inside the storefront.

He slipped on a pair of plastic shoe booties while Stone did the same with his articulated metal feet. They didn't pick up much, but anything that would save them time in the future was worth it. Zach pulled on a pair of purple gloves, and tugged his mask up into position. It wouldn't help with the smell, but it would help prevent him from sharing any DNA with the scene. That was one advantage Stone had—the mentic didn't need to worry about coughing on the scene, being a crystalized brain inside of a robotic body. As the junior detective, Zack waited for Stone to take the lead on the scene.

At two meters tall, Detective Stone looked imposing. His outer shell was reinforced blue with white stripes on the highlights. It gleamed even in the dim light from the yellowed lights above the entrance. Over it he wore a black, leather duster, an unnecessary affectation, but Zack understood he'd worn it back when he was meat and bone instead of being a dead can. His body was mostly human in shape, except the head, which was more of an assemblage of cameras and other electronics clustered around the titanium cranium housing the crystalized brain of Detective Stephen Newton, now ST-N3, or simply called "Stone." *Detective Stone* to the rookie detective and beat cops on the scene. Fifty years on the force and as a mentic he wouldn't be looking at retirement. *Ever.* Zack suppressed a shudder at the thought. He wasn't a religious or god-fearing man, never believed in all of that nonsense, but even he wouldn't want to become a mentic. *Immortality at that price? No thank you.*

"Let's see what we have," Detective Stone said, pushing open the door. The glass was backed by plywood nailed to the outside of the door, a faded sign calling it the "Kitty Kakes Bakery."

Grit and broken glass crunched beneath Stone's metallic footsteps as the mentic led the way inside. Zack followed, watching his steps as he lifted a flashlight and shone it around the scene.

Not much to see up front. A customer area was only about ten feet deep, two small tables bolted to the floor in front of the boarded over windows. A broken glass display case—the apparent source of the glass littering the floor—divided the front customer area from the staff area. At one time it would have held an assortment of Kitty's Kakes, presumably, but now it was like a gutted carcass, with bent metal ribs and smashed shelves. Multi-colored graffiti covered most of the walls, nonsense sprayed call signs and vulgarities. Ampules lay like shelled nuts on the floor, broken and empty.

Stone crouched smoothly, noiselessly, his duster pooling on the floor around him. He picked up one of the broken ampules between his finger and thumb and held it up. Zack saw flickers of green light as Stone's laser sampler licked out, tasting the molecules present.

"Crys," Stone said, his tone disgusted. He flicked the ampule back to the ground. "Oxidation more than a week. Not relevant right now."

Helpful to have a partner who is a walking lab, Zach thought.

He said, "If this is a usual place for someone to shoot up, they might have been surprised by the victim."

Stone rose to his full height. "If they're on crys, they won't have enough functional neurons for long to do anything. They don't normally turn violent."

"Sure." *Was it personal with Stone? Crys was the key chemical used in crystalizing brain tissue for mentics or other augmented computing platforms. It might touch a sore spot.*

"Come on." Stone walked around

the broken display case. "Uniforms said the body was in the back."

Zack followed. He hadn't heard anyone say that—but Stone could receive (and send) radio signals directly. Probably monitored all of the channels.

A narrow space behind the broken display case was littered with trash from fast food places. An open doorway led to a narrow hall, doors on each side, the one on the right open with light coming out of the room beyond. Zack clicked off his flashlight and followed Stone through into the bakery's kitchen. The body was immediately visible on the floor between a kitchen island (*missing the counter top*) and the empty shelves on the wall to his left.

The ceiling light panels left the scene in stark, clear relief. A torso, arms, legs, dismembered, lay on the floor in a clearly posed shape. Each limb arranged at right angles to the torso. One arm pointed up from where the head should have been, elbow at ninety degrees pointed right. Then a leg perpendicular to the torso, knee at ninety degrees pointing down. The remaining limbs mirrored those to create a recognizable swastika shape with the torso at the center. Light reflected off the torn metal, shredded wires and fiber optics. Zack let out his breath in relief. It was grisly, yes, but the body wasn't *human.*

"Is it a mentic?" he said.

Stone moved with smooth, graceful steps around the "body," following a spray-painted white circle around the remains. "Yes, undoubtedly. Look."

Zack followed Stone's pointing finger and saw what he had missed when he first took in the remains. At the center of the torso were what looked like two shiny metal bowls. *Not bowls.* It was the halves of a mentic's cranium, cut open. Each half filled with the pulverized green crystal shards of what had been—at one time—a human brain. What remained of the cushioning electroconductive fluid filled the bottom of the cranium sphere. *Now* his gut tightened, realizing truly what he was looking at here. It hadn't hit him at first. It looked like a bunch of machine parts, but this *person* had been a mentic, like his partner. Someone had dismembered them, laid out the parts in this obscene display, pried open the titanium brain case, and pulverized the crystalized brain inside. *Why?*

"Hey, Stone. Are you okay?"

Stone turned in his direction. There

wasn't a face to focus on, but Zack kept his attention on the black camera lenses and tried not to think *spider.*

"I'm fine. Are you, rookie?"

"Yeah, I'm good," Zack said. "I just meant—"

He stop himself, and shook his head. "Never mind. Let's get to work. This could be ritualistic. Someone who believes mentics are damned, right?"

Stone rose and moved with easy grace around the circle, then he stopped, crouching once again. He reached out to the remains, into the ripped open torso and pulled something from the wreckage. A spoon, the bowl blackened. A few charred and half melted green crystals clung to the metal.

"They tried to smoke their victim's brain."

"Smoke it?"

Stone rose back up to his full height. With his free hand he pulled an evidence collection bag from a pocket in his duster, dropping the spoon inside, sealing it. The tag shifted, e-ink displaying the details about when and where the item was collected.

Neat trick. Zack had to use his phone to write to the tags. Stone didn't have to bother with phones.

"Probably thought that they could extract crys from the pulverized brain tissue."

"That's not possible," Zack said, pretty sure he was right. Crys was used in the process to crystalize brain tissue, but it didn't remain afterward.

"No, it's not. Which explains why they left the remains behind and discarded their efforts."

Zack watched Stone, unable to read any expressions from the mentic. Hell, he wasn't even sure if Stone *had* emotions. It wasn't a mentic thing, mentics generally had the emotions and personality of the person they had been when alive. Stone was the way he was because of who *Detective Newton* had been when he was alive. Maybe becoming a mentic let Stone emphasize those traits? All Zack knew, from talk in the station, was that Stone was one of the most robotic and coldly logical detectives on the force. Even if Stone had an actual human face it probably wouldn't have shown any emotion as he studied the desecrated remains of another mentic.

"If all they wanted was to smoke the mentic's brains," (*that was a sentence he never thought he would say*) "then why go to all the trouble to dismember and pose the remains?"

Stone had slipped the bagged spoon into his right-hand pocket. Now he moved again, continuing his circuit of the body. Zack caught traces of reflected laser lights flickering across the remains.

"That is a valid point," Stone said after several seconds. "The damage isn't chaotic. They approached this methodically, dismembering and posing the remains in this symbol, painting the circle around it. The thigh joints and supports are cut back, shortening them to maintain a greater symmetry with the overall symbol. An organized killer. One who did this with a purpose."

"And didn't know that they couldn't smoke the brains?"

Stone had reached Zack's side again. "Apparently so, from the evidence at hand."

Zack moved away from the body, studying the rest of the kitchen. In several places the dust coating what was left of it had been recently disturbed. He made sure he didn't touch anything, taking his time to look around. He found a drawer on one side hanging halfway open. It still held a few odd utensils, including a couple spoons that looked like the one Stone had found.

"Stone, more spoons over here, looks like our crys junkie didn't bring the spoon with him."

Stone joined Zack at the drawer. "I see clear prints on the counter above the drawer, and on the back of the handle. I can get a high-resolution scan. I'll let the techs handle that."

"Good," Zack said. "Maybe we can close this case before lunch. Forty bucks says that the prints match a known offender."

"I'm not touching that bet," Stone said.

Zack didn't find anything else of a value. The door had been forced, they already knew that much. The property agent had entered with a key through the back door. She was next on his list to talk to.

"Can we get an id on the victim?" he said to Stone as they made their way back to the front to turn over the scene to the technicians.

"Yes," Stones deep voice said. "Identification is encoded in the A.I. core net that encapsulates the brain. Even with the damage, we should be able to extract that much. If the solid-state memory is undamaged we might get much more than just identification. The victim's memories might show us who killed them."

Final death. Mentics generally didn't die. That was kind of the point. Immortality, even though it came at a price. But they could die, as their victim discovered. No matter how tough the titanium cranium was, the crystalized brain inside, suspended in electroconductive fluid and wrapped in a core A.I. net, was vulnerable to damage. It took a lot to damage one, but it was possible. It couldn't be healed or repaired. Certainly not the pulverized remains that they had discovered. That person didn't exist any longer, even if there were digitally preserved memories.

Zack left Stone giving instructions to the cops and technicians that would officially document the scene, gather evidence, and run tests. Twenty years since the first mentic, and people still discriminated against them, refused to accept their humanity, but violence against mentics was usually rare. *Probably because they didn't feel pain the way blood and bone humans did. Not as satisfying if your victim doesn't hurt.*

Checking his notes on his phone, he

found the property agent's profile that dispatch had sent over.

Emma Harrison. Thirty-two. Pretty, in a serious, 'I mean business' way. The picture was from her license, and that usually didn't flatter anyone. She had dark hair, curly, touching her shoulders, with the outer ends dyed a bright metallic red. Small nose. Hazel eyes. A smattering of freckles across her nose and cheeks, not covered up. Her teeth didn't show in the picture, but the almost smirking smile did show two adorably cute dimples that made her look younger.

"The property agent," Stone said, over Zack's shoulder. "Pretty."

"Jeez!" Zack took a breath and stepped away from Stone, turning to look up at the mentic. "How do you manage to sneak up on people like that?"

"Talent," Stone said flatly. "Let's go."

CHAPTER 2
HARRISON

The door to Emma Harrison's walk-up was painted a fresh bright blue that put Zack in mind of tropical oceans. It was wide, deep-set, and rounded at the top with a brick archway above. The small area provided enough shelter for a couple people out of the rain—if it had been raining. A reinforced screen was dark on the right hand side wall beside the door. He'd gone up the steps first. Stone stood just outside the overhang, a dark presence in his duster. Zack looked up at him and tilted his head.

"You ever consider a hat? Something with a wide brim, you could pull it down low."

"That would interfere with my sensors."

"Well, maybe. You'd have to have

holes in it for your antennas at least, or it wouldn't sit right. It'd look amazing."

"I don't think so." Stone gestured at the wall panel. "Ring her?"

"Okay," Zack said. Ribbing the senior detective didn't seem to get a reaction.

He touched his fingertips to the screen. It came to life, showing an animation of scanning his fingerprints. The border flashed an amber color. A smooth female voice said, "The resident is currently unavailable. Would you like to leave a message?"

Zack shook his head. He pulled his badge off his belt and held it up so the camera could read the codes. "One of our officers dropped Ms. Harrison off. I'm Detective Wood, and that's Detective Stone behind me. We need to ask you a few questions, Ms. Harrison."

"One moment," the screen said. The amber border pulsed and rotated around the screen once, then twice. It pulsed again and turned green. "Ms. Harrison will be with you shortly."

Shortly ended up being about twenty seconds. Zack hadn't lost his patience yet. Most ordinary people—those not first responders—didn't normally deal with such things as the scene today.

The victim had been a mentic, but that didn't mean it wasn't an upsetting incident. He'd keep that in mind, be sympathetic. Stone would do whatever he wanted.

The woman opening the door didn't match the dimpled, smiling woman in her pic. Oh, it was her, obviously, but her expression was that of a person who was hitting the bottle early in the day after a particularly bad day. She sighed, looking at them on her stoop.

"Can't I just file my statement online? Do we have to drag this out? I don't know anything about what happened and I already turned over my files on the property."

Zack kept his face warm, but not overly bright. He didn't take it quite down to her level. *A comforting expression.* He'd been told that he had a kind face (*when he wanted to appear kind*), and reasonably good-looking. It usually worked well with witnesses, victim's families, and often even the suspects who thought that he was someone that *really understood* where they were coming from.

"Ms. Harrison, I understand. We received notification that you shared the files, thank you. I'm Detective Wood and this is Detective Stone."

Her eyes barely glanced over his shoulder at Stone, then back to him. She was only two years younger than himself. "So he's your boss, right?"

"Senior partner," Zack said, unperturbed. "Could we come in and speak with you about this morning? We won't take any longer than necessary. We need your help to catch the ones responsible."

Another glance past him at Stone, then back. "Stone and Wood, seriously? You're making that up."

He thought he saw the smallest hint of a crinkle at the corner of her eyes, a spark that hadn't been there a second earlier. "No, I'm afraid not. Just our luck. You can probably see why *I* could use your help."

The hint was subtle, but he wanted to establish a connection and help her open up about her recollections. Her memory would be most vivid today. The longer they waited the more details —insignificant or not—she would forget. They'd be down to whatever story she told herself over and over about this morning.

"Sure, come on in. I told the agency what happened. No one expected me to go back to work today, though I probably should have." She started walking into her building, leaving the door open. "It'd help keep my mind of it, and I'm going to have more to do to catch up after this. Not sure it's worth it."

"Thank you," Stone said, his deep voice carrying into the hall after her.

Ms. Harrison started, looking back quickly. She nodded. "Sure. Of course. I want to help."

Zack walked inside, suppressing a grin. Stone had that effect on people.

Her place was a simple two-story walk up. A stair a short distance inside climbed to a second floor, probably with a couple bedrooms and a bathroom. To their left, as they entered, an arched entryway led into a living room. Ms. Harrison led them down the short hall to a bright kitchen that gleamed with inexpensive stainless steel appliances and too-bright faux marble countertops. It was neat, though, and clean. A small breakfast nook (*in a space that was obviously beneath the stairs*), had two light blue chairs, though he guessed that the second wasn't often used.

"It's a nice place," he said.

Ms. Harrison walked around the small kitchen island to a coffee machine.

"Do you want coffee? I'm going to make some."

"That'd be nice, thank you."

With no place for them all to sit, Zack stood on one side of the kitchen island. Stone drifted over to two doors in the corner. Zack knew Stone's sensors would tell him if there was anyone else in the place.

Stone said, "You live alone, no pets."

It wasn't really a question, but Ms. Harrison said, "Right. Only me. Never met the right person."

She turned away at that last, focused on making coffee, adding a fresh canister. The machine was plumbed, no need to add water when it could take it right from the line.

Zack said, "Ms. Harrison, c—"

"Call me Emma," she said, turning. "If you want."

"Sure, Emma. Thank you. If you want to start, just tell us about this morning, starting from when you left home, what time was that?"

"Five past six. It only takes a couple minutes to get to the bus stop, it's around the corner. I don't drive. No need to, in the city."

Zack nodded. He took out an actual paper notebook, a pen, and jotted down the time. It wasn't necessary, even a bit wasteful, but he'd found it was what people expected. It didn't matter that Stone was a mentic and recording everything including Ms. Harrison's vitals, people felt more comfortable if he took notes and encouraged them.

"Orange line?"

"Right," she said. The coffee pot hissed and bubbled behind her, coffee starting to fill the carafe.

"Go on, Emma."

"Today was a typical day. I work remotely, from here, or sometimes I go out to a pub or cafe to work, you know? Mostly I go around to my assigned properties, I have a roster, and I go through each building to check on its condition. If I find any problems, I hire someone to come fix whatever is wrong. I document everything. If there is vandalism or a break in, I document that and call the police, plus I file a report with the office—I always file a report— but in a case like that there is a special report. I also create any insurance claims that we're going to need and file those."

"Tell us about today," Stone said. "Please go through what you did in detail, Ms. Harrison. A detail that seems inconsequential to you, might prove important to our investigation."

She nodded, turning back to the coffee machine as it sound a low tone. She reached up to a series of hooks beneath her wood cupboards (*painted a dark blue that contrasted with the bright counter tops*) where ceramic mugs hung. She took two down, looked back at him.

"How do you like your coffee?" She glanced over at Stone. "I don't know that I have anything to offer you, Detective Stone."

"You don't," Stone said. "Don't trouble yourself on my account."

"Black is fine," Zack said. "I'm watching my sugar intake."

"I can't do that," Emma said, making a face. "I like sugar and lots of milk in mine."

She poured coffee into a white and green mug with a saying on it, placing it down on the island in front of him.

"Deserve Today," read the saying on the side.

Good enough. Zack let the mug sit, wary of the steam billowing up, carrying the scent of a rich, dark roast.

She poured her own coffee, then turned around and leaned back against the counter, cradling a black coffee mug in her hands. It said, "Face it."

She said, "I left the house at my usual time, at five after six. I got to the bus stop, waited about a minute before it arrived, and got on. I rode the orange line into downtown, reading my book. It took me as far as water front and 13th, that's where I got off. I walked from there to the Shore street property."

"Point five two miles," Stone said.

Ms. Harrison glanced at him, lifting her mug to sip. When she lowered it she said, "Sure, about that, I guess. Close enough to walk. I don't mind."

"What time was it when you got off the bus?"

"Twenty after, about that. The transit line probably has records."

Stone didn't say anything.

"It was chilly this morning," Zack said, breaking the silence.

She shrugged one shoulder. "I don't mind it. It wasn't busy down there, usually isn't, especially that early. Nothing much to bring anyone down there and the smell drives away business. Who wants to shop, smelling that stink?"

Zack had no trouble remembering the odor of the low tide and the general stink of that part of downtown. He nod-ded, and waited for her to continue.

"I took the alley behind the property, using my key to unlock the back door. I went inside and started my inspection, and that's when I saw what had hap-pened in the kitchen. I didn't even know what I was looking at, initially. I thought it was some junk. Someone broke in and left a mess. Wouldn't be the first time."

Stone said, "Had anything else changed since your last inspection?"

"Some trash in the hallway. It smelled worse, someone had relieved themselves, I noticed that when I came in. I record footage as I do my inspec-tion so I can go back and compare."

"Was that footage included in the files you already shared?"

She shook her head. "I didn't think of it. I sent copies of my building re-ports. I take the videos to refer to, they aren't edited or anything."

Even better. Zach picked up the cof-fee. "Can you give us copies of your footage of the building? Today's and previous visits?"

He sipped the coffee, heat *almost* burning his lips. It had the slightly flat taste of lab-grown beans. Likely en-hanced caffeine content.

"Yes, of course."

He put the mug down. "When did you realize it was a body?"

"Body?" Emma straightened with a shake of her head. "I didn't. I mean, I didn't think of it like that. I—" she glanced at Stone "—thought it was some sort of hate speech. I didn't realize until I called the police and talked to someone, describing what I saw. When I told them about the green crystals, that's when they said it sounded like a mentic, told me not to touch anything, and to wait outside for the police. I went outside and waited like they said."

She took a drink of her coffee.

Zach picked up his and took another sip out of politeness.

Stone shifted his position. "I've sent you a link to a secure deposit. Please upload your recordings."

Emma's pocket buzzed and she started, put down her coffee, and took the phone out of her pocket. She looked up at Stone, then at Zach. "Right now?"

Zach said, "If you don't mind. We'd like to catch this murderer."

Her cheeks paled slightly. She chewed on her bottom lip, and tapped on her phone screen. "Of course."

Emma Harrison considered herself a

nice, unbiased person, Zach knew. His use of "murderer" had shaken her because she still had trouble thinking of this crime as murder. She didn't have a mentic partner. Probably rarely, if ever, encountered mentics in her day-to-day life. When she did, she would be polite, but wouldn't think of them as anything more than a machine. She was having trouble reconciling those views. He waited, watching her swipe and tap to upload the recordings, and sipped the coffee he didn't really want.

"That's it," she said, looking up, her voice showing both relief and irritation. "Is there anything else you need?"

Zach waited a couple beats for Stone to say anything if he wanted. When his partner didn't take the chance, Zach put down the coffee on the island. "No, I think that is everything. Thank you for your cooperation, and the coffee."

She pocketed her phone and crossed her arms. "You're welcome."

"Thank you, Ms. Harrison," Stone said.

Stone swept out of the kitchen with his usual grace, duster billowing slightly with the quick movement. Zach fought back a grin and followed his partner.

CHAPTER 3
VICTIM

t took nearly six hours for forensics to come back with an identification on their victim. The 'swastika murder' had taken a back seat to other cases for most of the day. They had gone back to the office after their interview with the property agent and settled in at their desks in the corner of the bullpen. They had a view with large windows on one side of the desks, sitting (or standing) back-to-back. Each had a worn bamboo top scuffed with use. Stone usually stood, having no physical need to sit down. Zach preferred his comfortable chair and leaned back, feet on the mostly empty desk, keyboard pushed back, with a pair of overlay glasses providing him with a large screen view.

Zach received the notification on the case channel and tapped it. Windows opened across his view with the forensic report. He took his feet from the desk and rocked forward.

"Are you seeing this?" he said.

"Interesting," Stone said. "We need to talk to the lieutenant."

"I think he's out right now, didn't he have that press conference?"

There was a pause for a second, then Stone said, "You're correct."

Zach took off the overlay glasses, leaving them on the worn bamboo surface, and stood up. "Let's go pick up Emma Harrison and bring her in for more questions."

"We don't have any reports back on the footage she shared," Stone said. "It might be premature to bring her in. We don't have anything to hold her on."

Zach shook his head. "Maybe not, unless she gives us something to go on, like a confession."

"You think she did it?"

"I don't have any other suspects," Zach said. "Do you?"

"No, but we haven't investigated all avenues yet. I'd rather have something else to go on. *And* make a stronger case to the lieutenant."

Zach sighed. He rubbed his chin, thinking. Stone wasn't wrong. It was a hunch in his gut, that's all, one he didn't understand. *Why would Emma Harrison butcher an unused mentic body and pose it in the building?* It didn't make much sense. And there had been the spoon, evidence that someone had tried to smoke the crystallized 'brain' inside—except it wasn't a crystallized human brain tissue at all. Forensics said it was waste product from crystallized tissue harvesting. Much of the robotics industry used portions of animal brains coupled with core A.I. nets to enhance the functionality of their machines. Those uses enhanced computational ability for tasks like vision recognition, without retaining any of the animal's behavioral or cognitive functions. Portions also assisted with other sensory recognition tasks and motor controls. The rest of the unused material was crushed and disposed of as waste.

Someone had gone to a lot of trouble to set up that scene. The swastika made from the dismembered mentic body, the open brain case, and the crystallized brain tissue had all been laid out. Meant to be seen. And there was a flaw in his logic.

Zach shook his head. "Why would she report it? She didn't need to call us."

Stone turned, facing Zach, which showed how interested his partner was in the conversation. Zach almost felt flattered.

"That is a good question," Stone said. "She called us about the scene. If she was responsible and wanted to keep it a secret, she wouldn't have called us."

"Or taken so much effort to stage it," Zach said. "Someone wanted that scene shown. It was created for an audience."

"I'm accessing her social streams."

Zach waited, knowing that Stone could complete the search much faster than he could do it.

"Look."

Zach's phone buzzed. He picked up the overlay glasses and slipped them on, opening the feed link that Stone sent over. He watched for several minutes before he pulled them off.

"Now do you want to go talk to her?"

"Yes," Stone said.

CHAPTER 4
CRIMINAL

Street feeds gave them Emma Harrison's position at a small cafe a couple blocks from her home, sitting outside at a ornate black metal table, beneath an umbrella that featured a butterfly pattern in shades of blue. She had a cup of coffee and an empty plate in front of her. Her attention was all focused on her phone. She didn't notice them until they reached her table, one on each side.

"Emma," Zach said, forcing a warmth he didn't feel into his voice. "I have a few more questions for you."

She started, then relaxed when she saw it was him. She cast a distrustful look at Stone, then back to Zach. "Detective Wood. I've told you everything already."

Her hand shifted, tilting the camera up. Her thumb tapped at the screen.

She was recording. Not surprising. It didn't matter. He wasn't concerned. "Not everything." He pulled out the chair at the side of the table and sat down. He leaned forward, bracing his hands on his knees.

"You said more on your feed," he said. "You're a good actor. It was almost believable."

"I don't have to explain anything to you," she said coolly.

Zach arched an eyebrow, looking over at Stone, then back to Ms. Harrison. He grinned. "You don't want to explain that among the properties you're assigned is a warehouse on the same street? A warehouse owned by Tentanya Industries and used to store mentic materials and supplies?"

She crossed her arms, glaring, lips pressed tightly together.

Zach said, "Our forensic team has already matched the body to material missing from Tentanya Industries' warehouse. And they've matched your DNA to both locations and the crys ampules we found."

"Of course my DNA is at both buildings! I'm the property agent!"

"Yes, but those ampules contained samples of your blood. We have a court order for a drug test. We'll find enough crys in your system to match to the residue left at the scene. You've been trying to grow your feed audience, giving them stories about the evidence of drug use and other crimes that you've found at your job. You wanted to escalate things, get more views, and the mentic parts gave you that chance."

She stood up abruptly. "I'm leaving."

Stone stepped up to her in one quick movement and gripped her upper arm. "Emma Harrison, I'm placing you under arrest for grand theft, fraud, and additional charges to be determined by the district attorney."

She yanked her arm, fruitlessly. "You can't! Let go!"

Zach stood up as Stone calmly read her her rights, leading the protesting Ms. Harrison to their car.

CHAPTER 5
HOME

The sound of Zach Wood's door closing out the world was the best thing in the world. He yawned and made his way through the dark apartment, not bothering with the lights. They'd picked up two more cases *after* bringing in Emma Harrison to be booked. The lieutenant was pleased that they'd managed to close the case quickly, even if it turned out not to be a homicide. It still looked good in their book.

Right now, though, all he wanted was sleep. It was late. A soft *meow* greeted him when he walked into the bedroom. "Lights ten percent."

Dim illumination rose in the corners of the room. From the second pillow, Lucy lifted her orange, white, and brown face, blinking sleepy green eyes at him.

"Hey there, Lucy, sorry about that. I'll turn the lights out in a second."

He sat on the edge of the bed to take off his shoes, comforted by Lucy's purring.

———

ABOUT THE AUTHOR

Ryan M. Williams is a full-time career librarian and a multi-genre writer with over twenty books. He writes across a range of genres including science fiction, fantasy, paranormal, mystery, horror, and romance. He earned a Master of Arts degree in writing popular fiction from Seton Hill University and a Master of Library and Information Science from San Jose University. His short fiction has appeared in Pulphouse Fiction Magazine, On Spec Magazine, and anthologies from Pocket Books and WMG Publishing.

ALSO BY
RYAN M. WILLIAMS

POEVILLE

The POEVILLE series with feline detective
C. Auguste Dupin and his human librarian
Penny Copper might be just the thing.

•The Murders in the Reed Moore Library

•The Task of Auntie Dido

MOREAU SOCIETY

Brock Marsden, a genetically-modified
detective, solves the toughest cases in a this
far future space opera series.

•Dark Matters

•The Gingerbread House

•Past Lives

•Past Dark

DEAD THINGS

Do you like your fantasy dark and
paranormal? Ravyn Washington isn't like
other students. Her grandmother was called
a witch and if the Inquisition discovers
Ravyn's abilities she could burn in the
DEAD THINGS series.

•Waking Dead Things

•Dreaming Dead Things

•Killing Dead Things

FILMING DEAD THINGS

Filming the Inquisition at work made Stefan Roland's ground-breaking documentary directing career—calling him the Jane Goodall of Dead Things.

•Farm of the Dead Things

•Mall of the Dead Things

•War of the Dead Things

•Trailer Park of the Dead Things

SCIENCE FICTION STORIES & NOVELS

Discover more science fiction with these books.

•Infestation

•Europan Holiday

•Stowaway to Eternity

•Crunch Bang: The Chrystal Eagle Stories

•Space Monkeys: A Short Science Fiction First Contact Story

•Invasion of the Book Snatchers: A Short Science Fiction Story of Small-Town Terror

ROMANCE BY KATE N. RYAN

And if you like romance and comedy, the books by KATE N. RYAN will tickle your funny bone—and more.

- Watching You Sleep: a laugh out loud romantic comedy

- Tom Scratch: A Short Fantastic Romance Story